Superphonics Storybooks will help your child learn to read using Ruth Miskin's highly effective phonic method. Each story is fun to read and has been carefully written to include particular sounds and spellings.

The Storybooks are graded so your child can progress with confidence from easy words to harder ones. There are four levels - Blue (the easiest), Green, Purple and Turquoise (the hardest). Each level is linked to one of the core *Superphonics Books*.

ISBN 0 340 80548 X

Text copyright © 2001 Clive Gifford
Illustrations copyright © 2001 Ian Cunliffe

Editorial by Gill Munton
Design by Sarah Borny

The rights of Clive Gifford and Ian Cunliffe to be identified as the author and illustrator of this work have been asserted by them in accordance with the Copyright,

First published in Great Britain 2001

10 9 8 7 6 5 4 3 2 1

First published in 2001 by Hodder Children's Books, a division of Hodder Headline Limited, 338 Euston Road, London

Printed by Wing King T

A CIP record is register

D0308446

Target words

This Turquoise Storybook focuses on the following sounds:

ar as in **farm** | **oi** as in **foil**

oy as in **boy** |

These words are featured in the book:

apart	far	parsnips
arm	faraway	party
arms	farmyard	scarf
barked	hard	Scarface
barn	hardly	Shark
Carl	harm	Sparko
Carl's	harness	star
cart	harvest	stars
cartloads	jar	started
charge	larder	varnish
charm	Margo	yard
chart	Margo's	yarn
dark	Mars	yee-har
darning	pardon	Zarg
darting	parking	

boy	asteroids	oil
cowboy	coil	oiled
Joy	Droid	soil
overjoyed	foil	voice
Roy	joined	
toy	joints	

(Words containing sounds and spellings practised in the Blue, Green and Purple Storybooks and the other Turquoise Storybooks have been used in the story, too.)

Other words

Also included are some common words (e.g. **have**, **over**) which your child will be learning in his or her first few years at school.

A few other words have been included to help the story to flow.

Reading the book

1 Make sure you and your child are sitting in a quiet, comfortable place.

2 Tell him or her a little about the story, without giving too much away:

A cowboy and a robot make friends, but the robot has places to go ...

This will give your child a mental picture; having a context for a story makes it easier to read the words.

3 Read the target words (above) together. This will mean that you can both enjoy the story without having to spend too much time working out the words. Help your child to sound out each word (e.g. **f-ar-m**) before saying the whole word.

4 Let your child read the story aloud. Help him or her with any difficult words and discuss the story as you go along. Stop now and again to ask your child to predict what will happen next. This will help you to see whether he or she has understood what has happened so far.

Above all, enjoy the stories, and praise your child's reading!

Ruth Miskin's Superphonics
Turquoise Storybook

Robot Roy

by Clive Gifford

Illustrated by Ian Cunliffe

Hodder Children's Books

a division of Hodder Headline Limited

Carl was a cowboy.

He had two cows, Joy and Margo.

In the summer, they lived out on the plains.

In the winter, they lived in the barn,

and Carl fed them on cartloads

of parsnips and corn.

One day, when he was digging the soil

and hoping for a good harvest,

Carl looked up into the sky.

"A shooting star!" he gasped.

A light was darting about in the sky.

As it hovered above the farm,

Carl saw that it was a spaceship!

He had to duck as it zoomed over his house

and landed in his yard!

It bumped along the ground.

It was going to hit the barn!

Carl shut his eyes.

Joy and Margo looked on in surprise.

They were glad it was spring

and they were not in the barn.

Out jumped a little man,
rubbing his metal joints.
Lights flashed on his head
and on his arms.

"Not my best bit of parking!
Oh – and sorry about your barn!"
he said.

"A toy robot!" cried Carl,

forgetting all about the barn.

"Got a black hole for a brain,

Earth boy? I'm not a toy!

My name is Roy-Zarg-Droid,

and I come from Planet Sparko!"

said the robot grandly.

"But you can call me Roy," he added.

The light on the robot's head flashed,
and his arm shot out to shake Carl
by the hand.

"My name is Carl the Cowboy,
and I'm in charge here!" said Carl.

"Pardon me for asking, Roy,
but what is a robot from Planet Sparko
doing in my farmyard?"

"Planet Sparko is far, far away.
I was on my way home from a party on Pluto
when I made a mistake with my star chart.
I should have turned right at Mars!"

"Let me show you the Star Shark," he went on.

"It's by far the fastest spaceship in the universe!"

He pulled Carl into the barn.

But the Star Shark was not looking its best.
It was full of holes.

"Anteating asteroids!" said Roy.

"Can I stay and fix it in your barn?"

Roy was in the barn for a long time.

He mended the Star Shark and brushed it
with varnish.

"When the varnish is hard,
the Star Shark will be as good as new,"
he told Carl. "But what I need now
is a jar of corn oil."

"Pardon me?" said Carl.

"A jar of corn oil – oh, and lots of butter!"

"It's not just the Star Shark that's cracked,"
said Carl to himself.

But he went to look in his larder.

He came back with his arms full of butter
(Margo's best) and a big jar of cooking oil.

"We need to make a runway
in your yard," explained Roy.

"First, Planet Sparko –

and then the universe!" cried Roy,

hopping into the Star Shark

and revving it up.

The spaceship started to slide

across the yard, faster and faster.

Carl watched with alarm

as it slithered down to the duck pond.

Splash!

Splosh!

Glug!

"Are you all right, Roy?" cried Carl.

A slimy, weedy thing crawled out of
the duckpond and joined Carl on the bank.

"Get away from me, or I'll call the Sheriff!"
barked Carl in his best cowboy voice.

"It's me, Roy!" said the thing.

"Quick, get me some oil, or my joints will rust!"

Carl found a can of oil in his cart.

They wiped off all the mud and weed,

and oiled Roy's joints.

"Thank goodness for my lucky charm!"
sighed Roy, gazing at the faraway stars.

"It's hardly lucky!" said Carl.
"You've crashed twice in one day!"

"Yes - but I came to no harm," said Roy.
"And in any case, those two dancing cows
of yours have given me a brainwave!"

Carl fetched a coil of rope and tied it
round Joy and Margo to make a harness.

The two cows pulled the Star Shark
out of the duckpond.

"Now we need some yarn and a long scarf!"
yelled Roy.

Carl fetched some darning wool and his best
cowboy scarf.

They loaded the Star Shark on to Carl's cart, and Joy and Margo pulled it to the foot of Scarface Hill.

Then they tied the scarf tightly between two trees.

Carl thought the Star Shark looked silly

perched on his old wooden cart.

But Roy was overjoyed!

He pressed a little ball of silver foil

into Carl's hand.

"Don't look until the Star Shark

and I are on our way to Planet Sparko!"

he said.

He hopped into the Star Shark.

Carl crossed his fingers

and kicked away the logs.

"We have lift-off!" cried Roy.

The cart hurtled up Scarface Hill.

At the top, Roy started up the Star Shark ...

... and it zoomed up into the air!

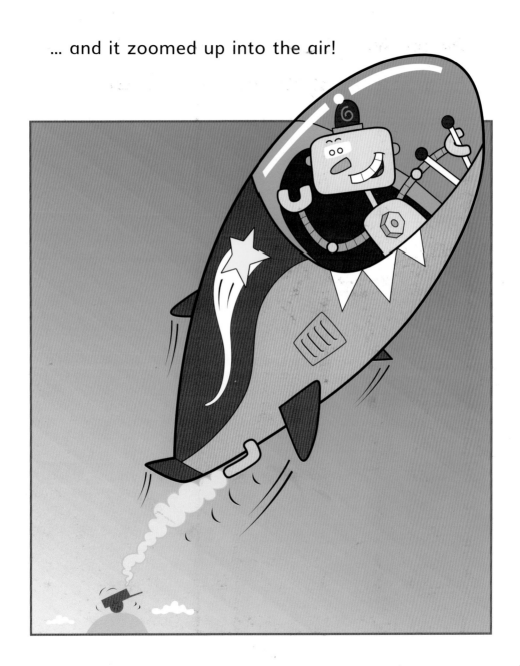

Alone on Scarface Hill,

Cowboy Carl looked at the little ball

of silver foil in his hand.

He pulled it apart.

It was Roy's lucky charm!

"Goodbye, Robot Roy!" said Carl,

looking up into the dark sky.

"Good luck on your trip back to

Planet Sparko!"